An Early I Can Read Book®

Hurray for Hattie Rabbit!

story and pictures
by Dick Gackenbach

HARPER & ROW, PUBLISHERS

Early I Can Read Book is a registered trademark
of Harper & Row, Publishers, Inc.

Hurray for Hattie Rabbit!
Copyright © 1986 by Dick Gackenbach

Library of Congress Cataloging-in-Publication Data
Gackenbach, Dick.
  Hurray for Hattie Rabbit.

  (An Early I can read book)
  Summary: Hattie Rabbit finds that mothers are
sometimes difficult and sometimes helpful.
  [1. Mothers and daughters—Fiction.   2. Rabbits—
Fiction]   I. Title.   II. Series.
PZ7.G1l7Hu 1986   [E]   85-45828
ISBN 0-06-021960-2
ISBN 0-06-021983-1 (lib. bdg.)

    1 2 3 4 5 6 7 8 9 10
         First Edition

For Doris Ritter Rutzel

Summer Bedtime

"Bedtime! It is bedtime!"
Hattie's mother called out.
When Hattie heard this,
she hid in the closet.
Hattie did not like
to go to bed
in the summertime.
The days are long
and the sky is still bright
and blue at bedtime.

Hattie's mother
found Hattie in the closet.
"Come out," she said.
"It is eight o'clock
and time for bed!"
"Oh," cried Hattie.
"Do I have to?"
"Yes!" said Mrs. Rabbit.
"You need your rest."
Hattie went upstairs to her room.
She put on her nightgown.
She could hear the birds
still singing in the trees.

6

"What an awful time
to go to bed,"
Hattie said to herself.

Hattie pulled down the covers

and got into her bed.

She fluffed her pillows.

She tossed

and she turned.

She pulled the covers over her head.

But nothing worked.

Hard as she tried,

Hattie could not fall asleep.

She got up

and sat on the edge of her bed.

"It is no use,"

Hattie said with a sigh.

Mrs. Rabbit walked into the room.

She was surprised

to find Hattie still awake.

"Why aren't you asleep?"

Mrs. Rabbit asked.

"You must be very tired.

You have had a busy day!"

"I am tired!"

Hattie told her.

"But I cannot sleep.

It looks like daytime in here."

"That is a problem,"

said Mrs. Rabbit.

10

"What can we do about it?"

"If only I could see the moon,"
said Hattie.

"And it would help
if I could see the stars too."

"Let me see what I can do,"
said Mrs. Rabbit.

Mrs. Rabbit left the room.

She came back with a shade,
some paint, and some brushes.

After Mrs. Rabbit hung the shade,
she painted a dark sky.

"Now paint the moon!"

said Hattie.

Mrs. Rabbit painted a moon.

"And do not forget the stars!"

Hattie reminded her.

Mrs. Rabbit painted twinkling stars.

"What else would you like?"

Mrs. Rabbit wanted to know.

"An owl in a tree,"

said Hattie.

Mrs. Rabbit painted a tree

with a night owl

perched on a branch.

Now the room was dark

and cozy.

"Who-oo-oo,"

whispered Mrs. Rabbit.

"Who-oo-oo should be in bed?"

Hattie did not answer.

She was sound asleep.

The Game

Hattie went to visit
her friend Rosie Pig.
Rosie had a frown on her face.
"What is the matter?"
Hattie asked her friend.
"I just asked my mother
for a gumdrop,"
Rosie told Hattie.
"What did she say?" asked Hattie.
"She said no!" Rosie replied.

"She said it would ruin my teeth."

"Well," said Hattie,

"mothers usually say no."

"You can say that again,"

said Rosie.

"I have a good idea,"

Hattie told Rosie.

"Let's play a game.

We will ask your mother questions.

The first one

to get her

to say yes wins."

"That sounds like fun,"

Rosie agreed.

"She is my mother,

so I go first!"

"Okay," said Hattie.

Rosie went into the kitchen.

"Mother," she said,

"may I go to the movies?"

"Not today," said Mrs. Pig.

22

Rosie returned to the porch.

"Mother said not today."

"Good try," said Hattie.

"Now it is my turn."

Hattie went into the house.

"Mrs. Pig," she said,

"may Rosie and I

have a pizza for lunch?"

"No," said Mrs. Pig.

"We have tuna fish."

Hattie told Rosie

what Mrs. Pig said.

"That was not even close,"

said Rosie.

"Let me try again."

Rosie picked a zinnia

and gave it to her mother.

"Thank you," said Mrs. Pig.

Then Rosie asked,

"Mother, may I have a party?"

"Maybe," said Mrs. Pig.

"How about on Saturday?"

Rosie suggested.

"I will have

to think about it,"

was Mrs. Pig's reply.

"Nice try," said Hattie.

"Oh," cried Rosie.

"Let's give up!"

"Not yet," said Hattie.

"Give me one more chance.

I can make her say yes.

I just know it."

Hattie went

to see Mrs. Pig again.

Rosie waited.

She wondered

what Hattie had in mind.

Soon, Hattie called

from the kitchen.

"Come on in, Rosie.

Your mother said yes."

Rosie was delighted.

She ran

as fast as she could.

Mrs. Pig was all smiles.

Rosie pulled Hattie aside.

"What did you ask her?"

she whispered to Hattie.

"I asked your mother,"

said Hattie,

"if we may brush

our teeth."

"Oh," moaned Rosie.

"Blah and phooey."

"Don't complain,"

said Hattie.

"It worked

and I won!"

Before they brushed
their teeth,
Mrs. Pig gave them each
a gumdrop.